Anthony Browne

WILLY THE CHAMP

WALKER BOOKS

AND SUBSIDIARIES

LONDON • BOSTON • SYDNEY

First published 1985 by Julia MacRae Books.

This edition published 1996 by Walker Books Ltd
87 Vauxhall Walk, London SE11 5HJ

2 4 6 8 10 9 7 5 3

© 1985 Anthony Browne

Printed in Hong Kong

British Library Cataloguing in Publication Data
A catalogue record for this book is available
from the British Library.

ISBN 0-7445-4356-8

For Ellen

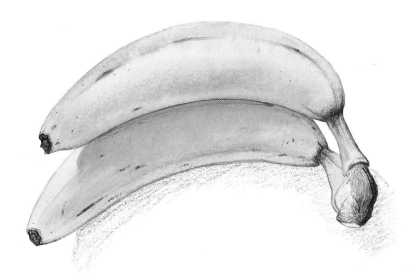

Willy didn't seem to be any good at anything.

He liked to read . . .

and listen to music . . .

and walk in the park with his friend, Millie.

Willy wasn't any good at soccer . . .

He did try.

Willy tried bike racing . . .

He really did try.

Sometimes Willy walked to the pool.

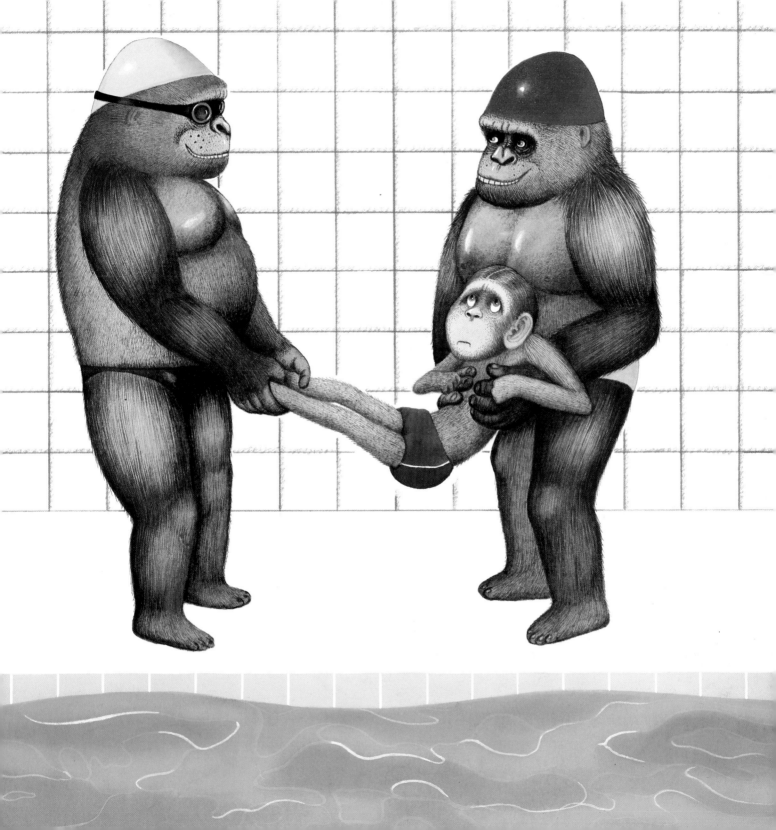

Other times he went to the cinema with Millie.

But it was always the same. Nearly everyone
laughed at him – no matter what he did.

One day Willy was standing on the corner with
the boys when a horrible figure appeared.

It was Buster Nose.
And he *had* a horrible figure.
The boys fled.

Buster threw a vicious punch.

Willy ducked . . .

. . . then he stood up!

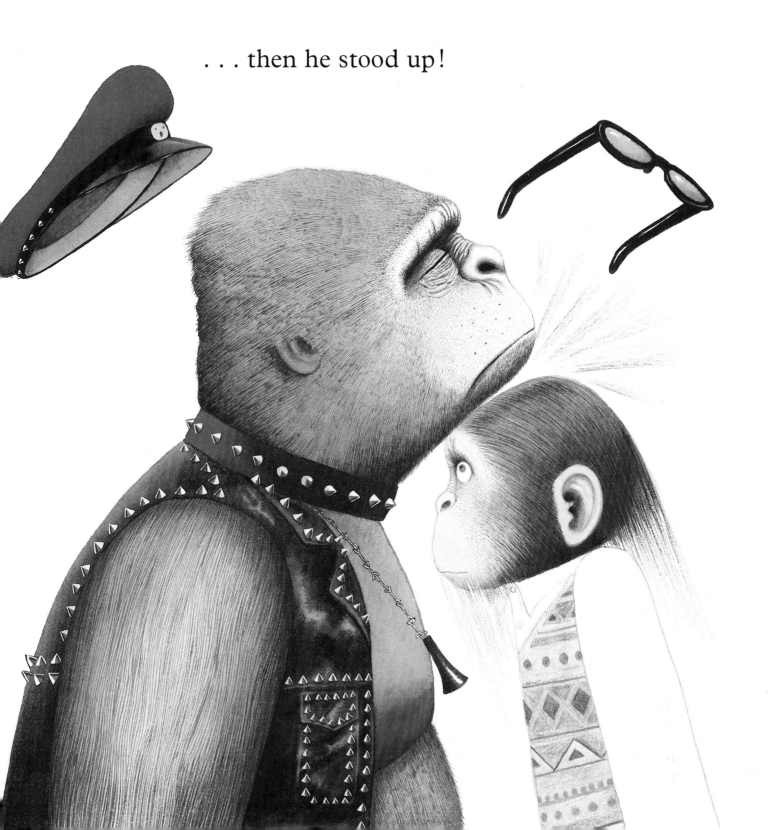

"Oh, I'm sorry," said Willy, "are you alright?"

Buster went home to his mum.

Willy was the Champ.